Pokémon

JUNIOR HANDBOOK

PIKACHU AND PALS

BY SIMCHA WHITEHILL

Ready to discover the world of Pokémon? Inside this book you'll meet some of the cutest, most popular Pokémon in the Sinnoh Region. Just turn the page to start your Pokémon quest.

ISBN-13: 978-0-545-15703-2
ISBN-10: 0-545-15703-X

12 11 10 9 8 7 6 5 4 3 2 1   9 10 11 12 13 14/0

Designed by Kay Petronio
Printed in the U.S.A.
First printing, August 2009

SCHOLASTIC INC.

New York   Toronto   London   Auckland   Sydney
Mexico City   New Delhi   Hong Kong   Buenos Aires

MEET THE POKÉMON TRAINERS

ASH

Ash Ketchum is a Trainer who wants to become a Pokémon Master! His best buddy, Pikachu, is always by his side.

BROCK

Brock is a Trainer of Rock-type Pokémon. He and Ash have been pals for a long time.

DAWN

Dawn is a Coordinator who is just beginning her Pokémon journey. She is a new friend to Ash and Brock.

Jessie, **James**, and **Meowth** are Pokémon thieves! They steal Pokémon from other Trainers. Luckily, they aren't very good at it.

TEAM ROCKET

AZURILL
POLKA DOT POKÉMON

The bouncy ball at the end of Azurill's tail is full of food. It helps Azurill hop around.

How to say it: *ah-zoo-rill*

Type: Normal

Height: 0'08"

Weight: 4.4 lbs.

An adorable Azurill lives in Mr. Backlot's mansion.

BIDOOF

PLUMP MOUSE POKÉMON

 **FUN FACT** Ash and Brock once helped save a bunch of wild Bidoof from an angry Steelix.

BONSLY
BONSAI POKÉMON

STATS

When Bonsly cries, it's not because it's sad. It's just sweating off extra water.

How to say it:
BON-sleye

Type: Rock

Height: 1'08"

Weight: 33.1 lbs.

FUN FACT

Bonsly might be small, but it's strong! Brock's Bonsly once busted itself out of a Team Rocket cage.

BUDEW
BUD POKÉMON

In spring, Budew's red and blue buds open up and release a pollen that will make you sneeze. *Achoo!*

How to say it:
bud-DOO

Type: Grass/Poison

Height: 0'08"

Weight: 2.6 lbs.

FUN FACT

Early in his Sinnoh journey, Ash spotted a bright Sunny Day move. When he followed the light show, he met Budew.

BURMY
BAGWORM POKÉMON

Trash Cloak

Sandy Cloak

Plant Cloak

STATS

Burmy can change their cloaks for different battles. They have sandy cloaks on the beach, plant cloaks in the woods, and trash cloaks in buildings.

How to say it:
BURR-mee

Type: Bug

Height: 0'08"

FUN FACT   A male Burmy can evolve into Mothim.

CHERUBI
CHERRY POKÉMON

Cherubi's tiny head stores healthy food. The food tastes as sweet as candy.

How to say it:
chuh -ROO-bee

Type: *Grass*

Height: *1'04"*

Weight: *7.3 lbs.*

Gardenia, the Eterna City Gym Leader, has a special Cherubi she takes everywhere she goes.

8

CHIMCHAR
CHIMP POKÉMON

Even rain can't put out the fire on the end of Chimchar's tail.

How to say it:
CHIM-char

Type: Fire

Height: 1'08"

Weight: 13.7 lbs.

Ash's Chimchar originally traveled with his rival, Paul. But it was happy to become part of Ash and Pikachu's family.

9

COMBEE

TINY BEE POKÉMON

Combee's Enchanted Honey is made from the nectar of a Pomeg flower. The honey's smell attracts all Pokémon.

How to say it:
COHM-bee

Type: Bug/Flying

Height: 1'00"

Weight: 12.1 lbs.

10

FUN FACT In the Eterna Forest, thousands of Combee have formed a wall to guard Vespiquen and the Amber Castle.

CRANIDOS
HEAD BUTT POKÉMON

Cranidos were extinct for a hundred million years. Scientists brought Cranidos back to life by cloning its fossils.

How to say it: CRANE-ee-dose	
Type: Rock	
Height: 2'11"	
Weight: 69.4 lbs.	

FUN FACT Cranidos once fought Team Rocket so fiercely, it evolved into Rampardos.

CROAGUNK
TOXIC MOUTH POKÉMON

STATS

When Croagunk's second finger turns purple, it can use the poison in its cheeks to jab its enemies.

How to say it:
CROH-gunk

Type: Poison/Fighting

Height: 2'04"

Weight: 50.7 lbs.

12

A Croagunk followed Meowth home one day, but Team Rocket decided to leave it behind. So Croagunk found a new friend in Brock.

GLAMEOW
CATTY POKÉMON

STATS

Glameow can use its beautiful eyes to hypnotize its enemies.

How to say it:
GLAM-ee-ow

Type: Normal

Height: 1'08"

Weight: 8.6 lbs.

Coordinator Zoey enters Contests and battles with her best buddy, a gorgeous Glameow.

HAPPINY
PLAYHOUSE POKÉMON

Happiny like to keep oval stones in their pouches. The stones make these cheerful Pokémon look more like Chansey.

How to say it: *hap-PEE-nee*	
Type: Normal	
Height: 2'00"	
Weight: 53.8 lbs.	

Brock and Croagunk won a Pokémon Egg at a Pokémon Dress Up Contest. When the Egg hatched, Happiny was inside!

MANAPHY
SEAFARING POKÉMON

STATS

Manaphy's body is eighty percent water! That makes this Legendary Pokémon a very good swimmer.

How to say it:
MAN-uh-fee

Type: Water

Height: 1'00"

Weight: 3.1 lbs.

FUN FACT

Manaphy will swim across whole oceans to return to its home beneath the sea.

MANTYKE

KITE POKÉMON

STATS

Mantyke is a very fast swimmer. The patterns on its back reveal what Region it comes from.

How to say it:
MAN-tike

Type: Water/Flying

Height: 3'03"

Weight: 143.3 lbs.

FUN FACT

When Pikachu and its friends accidentally sailed out to sea, Ash, Dawn, and Brock rode a Mantyke to rescue their Pokémon.

PIKACHU
MOUSE POKÉMON

STATS

When Pikachu are being cautious, their chubby red cheeks release an electric charge.

How to say it: *PEE-ka-choo*	
Type: Electric	
Height: 1'04"	
Weight: 13.2 lbs.	

Ash and his Pikachu are best friends. Ash even trusted Pikachu to decide whether it wanted to evolve into Raichu. But Pikachu was happy being Pikachu!

17

PIPLUP
PENGUIN POKÉMON

 FUN FACT

How did Dawn become friends with her Piplup? She rescued it from an attack by the fierce Pokémon Ariados!

SHAYMIN
LAND FORME
GRATITUDE POKÉMON

STATS

Shaymin uses the flowers on its back to clean the world around it. It can turn pollution into water and light.

How to say it:
SHAY-min

Type: Grass

Height: 0'08"

Weight: 4.6 lbs.

Shaymin Land Forme is very shy. It makes flowers bloom on its back when it's happy.

19

SHELLOS
SEA SLUG POKÉMON

East Sea

West Sea

STATS

The Shellos of Sinnoh come in two colors depending on where they live — pink for West Sea and blue for East Sea.

How to say it:
SHELL-oss

Type: Water

Height: 1'00"

Weight: 13.9 lbs.

FUN FACT

Dawn's friend Zoey caught her pink pal Shellos in the same lake that Ash met his buddy Buizel.

SHIELDON
SHIELD POKÉMON

FUN FACT

When Pokémon Hunter J tried to poach a pack of Shieldon, Ash and his old rival, Gary Oak, teamed up to rescue them.

SHINX
FLASH POKÉMON

22

FUN FACT Ash's friend from Jubilife City, Landis, has a Shinx that can tell if a Pokétch bracelet is real or fake.

STARLY
STARLING POKÉMON

Starly's strong wings help it blast off like a rocket ship!

How to say it:
STAR-lee

Type: Normal/Flying

Height: 1'00"

Weight: 4.4 lbs.

FUN FACT When Team Rocket stole Ash's Starly, Starly escaped from its cage and helped other Flying-types escape, too.

TURTWIG

TINY LEAF POKÉMON

When Turtwig drinks water, the shell on its back becomes hard.

Pronounced:
TUR-twig

Type: Grass

Height: 1'04"

Weight: 22.5 lbs.

FUN FACT Ash's Turtwig is very loyal. It protects other Pokémon from thieves like Team Rocket.